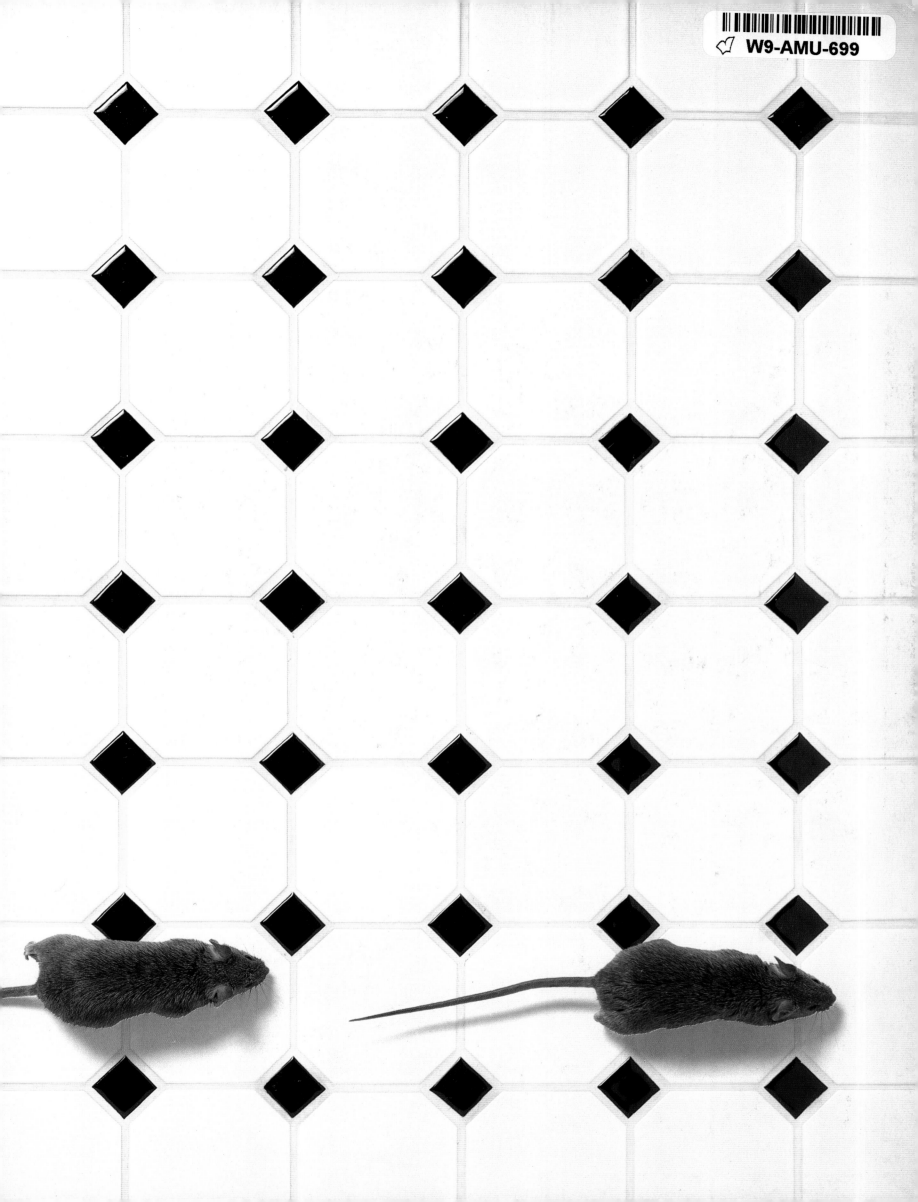

A DORLING KINDERSLEY BOOK

Managing Editor Jane Yorke
Editor Andrea Pinnington
Design by Mark Richards
Photography by Tim Ridley
Production Marguerite Fenn

Dorling Kindersley would like to thank Liz Button, David Corke,
Hilary Foster, Intellectual Animals, Christine Joslin, The Lighthouse,
Gatto Pavone, and Carolyn Russell for their help in producing this book.

First published in Canada in 1991 by
STODDART PUBLISHING CO. LIMITED
34 Lesmill Road, Toronto, Canada M3B 2T6

Third printing October 1993

ISBN   0-7737-2526-1

Manufactured in Italy

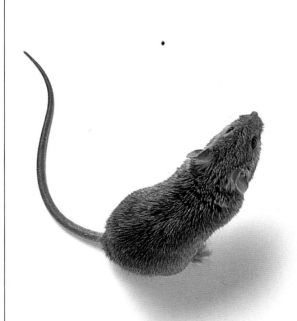

A MOUSE IN THE HOUSE

by
Henrietta

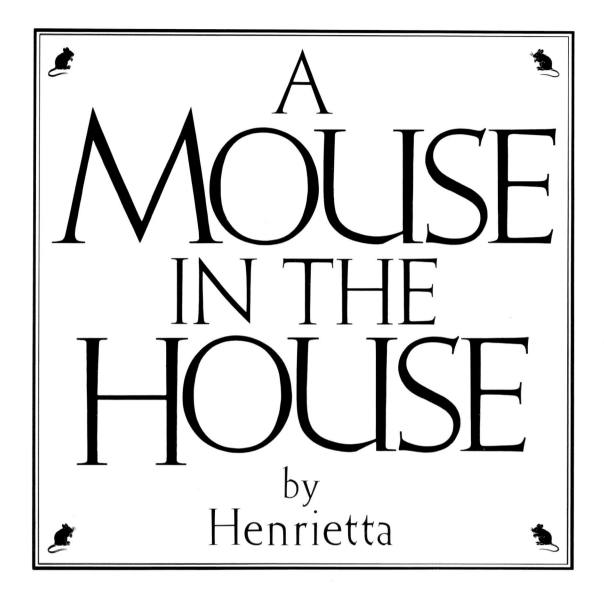

Stoddart

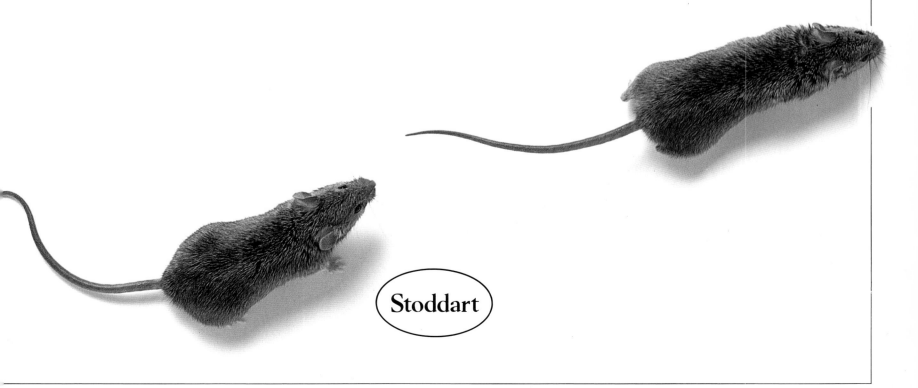

Today is a birthday! Today is a treat!
Some friends are invited to play and to eat.

The house is all ready, balloons at the door,
But no one has seen me down here on the floor.

I wasn't invited, but I'll be a guest,
At this birthday party along with the rest.

On each page, in each room, I'll be doing my worst.
Can *you* find me hiding? Will cat find me first?

There are lots of nice things that may look like a mouse,
But there's only one *me*, a *real* mouse in this house.

7

Garden room first, where I nibble my way
Through presents well-hidden for this special day.

8

*K*itchen shelves next! There is coffee and tea
And cheese left uncovered, just waiting for me.

*K*itten-shaped cookies, ready to bake,
A taste of the icing, now I'll try the cake!

12

Gifts in the hallway, coats in a heap,
I can hide safely while cat is asleep.

The party is swinging, the candles are blown,
While I've had a fabulous feast of my own!

16

Now to the playroom to play with the toys.
But where are the girls? And where are the boys?

*N*o one is watching, so I'll just explore.
Oh dear! Teddy's stuffing is spilled on the floor!

There's a boat in the bathroom that I'd like to sail.
But now I'm all wet from my nose to my tail!

*N*ighttime is coming—I'll soon go upstairs,
But first wait for Teddy to have his repairs.

On to the attic, the best is for last!
No one comes up—I can hide in the past.

26

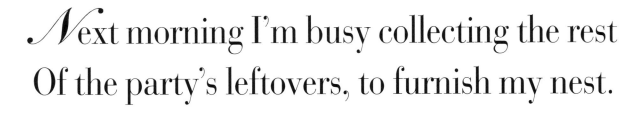

Next morning I'm busy collecting the rest
Of the party's leftovers, to furnish my nest.

I've explored every room to find every scrap,
And now that I'm finished, I'll stop for a nap.

I see paws at the door! The cat seeks a mouse.
I may have to move on—is there room in *your* house?